# MONTE CASANOVA

For Celeste and Altair.

MONTE CASANOVA

A modern tragedy in two acts

by Tutafarel

*Seventh Press*

2025

ISBN: 979-8-218-76249-0

Library of Congress Control Number: 2025917472

Edited in Los Angeles, CA.
First published in 2025 by Seventh Press.

# MONTE CASANOVA

# DRAMATIS PERSONAE

MONTE CASANOVA — A fallen icon drawn into the ruins of his sister's political legacy. Haunted, idealistic, and learning too late how power works.

TRINITY CASANOVA — His twin sister. A revolutionary presence whose absence defines the world she left behind.

NICO SERRANO — Monte's speechwriter. Quiet, watchful, more strategic than he lets on.

DETECTIVE — A sharp investigator. Unsentimental, deliberate, and quick to follow the scent of something off.

CHORUS — Journalists, influencers, and digital spectators. The voice of the crowd, the archive, the algorithm.

# TIME & PLACE

A far-future version of Los Angeles, now the capital of a fractured republic. The world is post-crisis, post-plague, and ruled by image, digital memory, and control.

Skyscrapers stream propaganda in ambient light. Grief has been monetized. Faith is algorithmic. The past is rebranded nightly, and silence is more suspicious than sin. This is a city where visibility equals survival, and forgetting is a form of compliance.

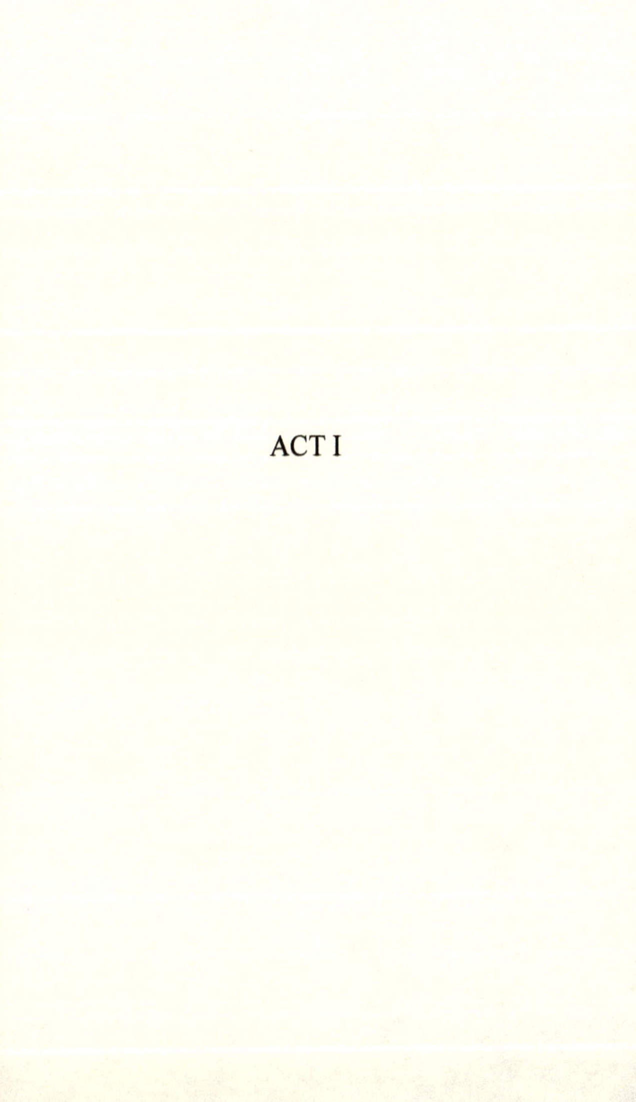

# ACT I

# <u>SCENE I</u>

*A square of figures, center stage. Still. Upright. Each holds a glowing phone. A single white LIGHT shines directly above them, harsh and holy. They do not look at one another. They read. Their voices rise together — slow, deliberate, spell-like.*

*At the very front of the stage, just inside the downstage line, a nearly invisible scrim hangs where a curtain might once have been. It is not yet lit.*

CHORUS

We are the ruins left behind. The echoes underwater. The last breath from Mother Earth. We lived through the fever. We buried the names. We watched the skies turn black, and we memorized the sound of silence. We are the after. The record. The rust in the wires. The weight that memory leaves behind.

*A faint hum begins beneath them — mechanical, ancient, like a system booting up.*

CHORUS

She believed it could be fixed. She drafted
maps. She outlined futures. They called it
strategy. We called it hope.

*A soft glow appears on the scrim. A hologram
of TRINITY CASANOVA begins to form — still,
upright, not yet fully rendered. The image
sharpens slowly as the CHORUS continues.*

CHORUS

Trinity Casanova. She gave them a blueprint.
Not a campaign. Not a brand. An actual plan.
They took it. They changed the margins. Then
they let her die.

*Her image is clear now lifelike, composed,
luminous. Too luminous.*

CHORUS

"It was an accident." "It was a glitch." "It was a
virus." "It was a necessary loss." The press
wrote poems. The state named a wing after her.

*TRINITY flickers — glitching once, then again
— and vanishes from the scrim without a trace.*

CHORUS

And one week later, they asked him to speak.

*A shift in tone. More voices join — layered,
overlapping, like memory rebooting.*

CHORUS

The plague came. The father fell. The girl was
lost. And the boy remained.

*As the following line begins, the scrim re-
illuminates — this time with floating digital
detritus: headlines, corrupted files, blurred
articles, fragments of commentary. They glitch
and flicker in sync with the voices.*

CHORUS

We do not mourn the adorned. We do not pity
the crowned. They feasted while we starved.
They built palaces atop our graves. Their
beauty was bought with our blood. Their
elegance, a veil for our chains.

*The flickering fragments continue, fading in
and out like corrupted newsfeeds:
"Grief or Grab for Power?"
"Crisis Cosplay"
"A Man Without a Plan"*

*A pause. The LIGHT flickering slows. The
CHORUS lowers their heads slightly, still
holding their phones, as their final words rise.*


CHORUS
This is the story of a state that mistook a man
for a promise. And when his sister's death left a
silence, they built a podium on her grave.

*A final silent glitch pulses across the scrim —
like a last system failure.*

*Then: BLACKOUT.*

*The white LIGHT above the CHORUS FADES.
They walk out in silence, their phones still lit.
One by one, the phones go dark — like stars
going out, or memories being forgotten.*

*In the darkness, the scrim rises and disappears.
Sudden sound: camera flashes. Fast. Chaotic.
LIGHT stutters across the stage. Flashbulbs
erupt. The stage LIGHTS cut harsh and cold.*

*Enter MONTE CASANOVA. He walks with
practiced grace, though his shoulders carry*

*weight. He stands beneath the LIGHT, the
podium rising to meet him.*

MONTE

I am not here to mourn her. I am here to finish
what she began. This initiative is not symbolic.
It is structural. Restitution in the form of
housing, clean air, and rebalanced labor grids.
Public systems that serve the public. Legacy
means nothing without execution.

I do not stand here as a shadow of my father. I
stand here in the wreckage of his architecture,
and I say we must build again, but from the
truth.

I'm tired of living in a city built on lies. I'm
tired of turning a blind eye and holding on to
expectations of a better future, one that was
modeled after a broken past and a corrupted
economic system. I'm tired of brushing off
discomfort, and I invite you to join me.

*A loud noise of a camera shutter, followed by a
bright flash of LIGHT. All characters freeze.
The stage is now lit by a single BACKLIGHT,
painting a tableau of frozen silhouettes.*

*A chorus of clicks, reporter walla, and
fragmented speech begins to rise — not from a
single body, but from all corners of the room.*

CHORUS
*(unseen, overlapping)*
He inherited power without any credibility.
Same old greedy name...
I liked him better before the politics.
Another playboy businessman?
Ugh, his sister was so much better.
I wonder who wrote this one...

*The voices blend and bleed — news alerts,
digital captions, real-time interpretations. The
Chorus is not one voice, but many.*

*As the following lines begin, the stage LIGHT
slowly returns to its original setup, taking us
away from the freeze-frame and back to the
present.*
CHORUS
He gives them language. They give him
mirrors. He moves with care. They move faster,
in cycle. His mouth opens, only so they can
write what he meant to say.

*The LIGHTS are fully back on. The characters unfreeze. MONTE steps back slightly from the podium. A REPORTER steps forward from the gallery. She's young, sharp, smiling, and already live-streaming from her phone.*

REPORTER (CHORUS EMBODIMENT)
You speak of action and blueprints, yet you hold no official title. Are you positioning yourself as some sort of moral savior or quietly launching a campaign built on collective grief?

MONTE
I speak because silence has failed us.

*The CHORUS hums faintly. A final flash goes off, lingering like static. MONTE remains still. He does not exit. The LIGHT remains on him as the voices reassemble beneath.*

CHORUS
*(final, distant)*
He says it well. But he says it late. He speaks like the dead are still listening.

*LIGHTS FADE.*

*End of Scene.*

<u>**SCENE II**</u>

*A holding chamber behind the forum stage. Sleek, clinical. One wall flickers with a silent feed: headlines, poll responses, red-tinted thumbs crawling upward and down.*

*MONTE removes his jacket, places it over a bench. He does not sit.*

*Enter NICO SERRANO. Dressed clean. Observing. He shuts the door behind him.*

NICO

You hit your marks.

MONTE

Marks don't matter if they're not remembered.

NICO

They'll remember. They'll argue, then they'll repost. Then they'll forget they doubted you.

MONTE

Do you think I'm here to be reposted?

                    NICO

I think you're here because the system needs
your face. And because you still believe it can
be changed.

                    MONTE

Do you not?

                    NICO

I believe change is expensive.

*Pause.*

                    NICO

And that you're paying for it in full view of
people who'd rather watch than help.


                    MONTE

They don't have to help. They just have to
listen.


                    NICO

Well, they won't do that. And you know it. But
you go out there anyway.


*MONTE glances toward the screen. A new
headline scrolls across in real time:*

*"Monte Casanova: Vanity or Redemption?"*

NICO

They don't hear your words. They hear the
myth. Casanova. Resurrection. You know it's
all a performance, you just have to keep them
entertained... Hopeful.


MONTE

Oh, come on, you know I'm done playing to
please.


NICO

And you perform that so beautifully!

*Silence.*

*MONTE crosses the room in annoyance as he
pulls out a vape from his pocket and takes a
heavy hit. He looks away from NICO, staring at
the newsfeed on the screen.*


MONTE

Do you think I don't know how they see me?


NICO

I think you know too well. And you still think
you can outtalk it.

*Silence.*

MONTE

If I don't speak, I vanish.


NICO

Then maybe you should vanish. At least for a while —


MONTE

That's not who I am.

NICO

*(quiet)*

Well then, maybe that's the problem. You can't just take, take, take, and never give —

*MONTE turns and gives NICO a look that cuts him off. Something passes between them, a tension that has lasted days.*

MONTE

You're not subtle anymore.

NICO

Yeah. I'm tired.

MONTE

Tired of me?

NICO

Of pretending it's not killing you.


*A pause.*

*NICO walks past him. The feed reflects both their silhouettes. NICO hits a button hidden on the wall, and the large screen turns off. The LIGHT in the room is now soft, and the air between them is much lighter, like a sigh.*

NICO

You could have rebuilt quietly. Let them forget you for a while, and then return on your own terms.

MONTE

There's no return for people like me. There's no leaving. I can't take a vacation from who I am, Nico, I-

NICO

Okay, okay, relax. Take a deep breath...

*MONTE looks away. The silence swells. Not angry, but familiar. Inevitable.*

MONTE

I meant what I said.

NICO

I know. That's what makes it tragic.

*MONTE exhales. NICO starts to leave. He pauses at the door.*

NICO

For what it's worth... You're still the best speech I've ever written.

*He exits.*

*MONTE remains, alone with the screen. He turns it back on. One last headline scrolls past: "Casanova Back on Top? Place Your Bets."*

*LIGHTS FADE.*

*End of Scene.*

# <u>SCENE III</u>

*A quiet, dim study. Floor-to-ceiling shelves. A large, clean desk. Plants are dead, but still upright in their pots.*

*MONTE enters quickly, a vape in his hand. He doesn't linger. He goes straight to the desk. Opens drawers. Shuffles folders. He is searching, focused. Not emotional. He pulls open a side drawer and stops.*

*MONTE grabs a small notebook from the drawer and flips through the pages. He stops and stares at a specific page. His hand lingers on the paper. Then —*

*A soft shift in LIGHT. The room warms, as if touched by a halo.*

*TRINITY enters. Not as a ghost, but as memory made present. She is mid-sentence, already walking toward the desk.*

TRINITY

If you quote me, you owe me breakfast. I want to see you say that line with jam on your face.

                    MONTE
You hated breakfast.

                    TRINITY
I hated you at breakfast.

*MONTE exhales — almost a laugh. Almost.*

                    TRINITY
You're back here again?

                    MONTE
I was looking for something.

                    TRINITY
You always are.

                    MONTE
You used to say that like it was a flaw.

                    TRINITY
No. I used to say it like it was exhausting.

*A beat.*

                    TRINITY
                    *(soft)*
It's what makes you dangerous.

MONTE

Then why are you the one they buried?

TRINITY

Because I said it without smiling. Because I didn't look like someone they could market. Because I didn't wait for their permission to speak.

MONTE

And I do?

TRINITY

You don't wait. But you think they listen, that's your weakness. You still want to be understood.

*MONTE looks away.*

MONTE

I quoted you tonight.

TRINITY

I know. You paused too long before the line, though.

MONTE

Oh my God, even dead you're annoying!

                    TRINITY

I'm just saying, kinda looked like you forgot
what you were going to say...


*TRINITY clocks the vape in his hand.*


                    MONTE

I didn't forget! I paused.


                    TRINITY

But you know your voice got all raspy toward
the end, right?


                    MONTE

No, it didn't!


*She snatches the vape from his hand mid-
sentence, takes a hit, and finishes the sentence
holding the vapor in:*


                    TRINITY

Yeah, it did. The Valley girl jumped out. I was
waiting for you to go like —


*She flips her hair jokingly as she exhales a puff
of vapor directly into his face, playful but
pointed:*

                    TRINITY
          (mocking, Valley girl affect)
"Literally."

                    MONTE
       (snatching the vape back, mocking)
Lit-rally.


*They laugh. MONTE takes another hit from the
vape.*


                    TRINITY

You flinched.


                    MONTE
           (exhaling vapor)

I breathed!


                    TRINITY

Okay, so you flinched and you breathed.


*Soft chuckles. She moves to the desk, facing
away from MONTE.*


                    TRINITY

They'll offer you the same choice they offered
me: be worshipped or be erased. And you'll
want to believe there's a third option.

*Pause.*

TRINITY

There isn't.

MONTE

Then what do I do?

TRINITY

*(approaching MONTE, anger rising)*
You speak. Be loud, messy. Become impossible to forget. Show them that you won't die in silence like I did, make them pay for the plague our name will forever carry —

*MONTE abruptly closes the notebook, and the LIGHTS immediately shift back. TRINITY goes silent.*

*She slowly walks off stage, fading in silence, like a memory being put away.*

*MONTE remains by the desk. He sits down. Alone again. He contemplates next to the dead plants as the LIGHTS SLOWLY FADE.*

*End of Scene.*

<u>**SCENE IV**</u>

*The stage fractures into zones: half-lit vignettes of digital communication — a couch, a bed, a desk, a car, a TV studio... Scrolling feeds play across the scrim. LIGHTS flicker onstage, revealing and obscuring new scenes.*

*The CHORUS takes form: journalists, podcast hosts, political commentators, influencers, neighbors, classmates, strangers on the train. Some speak from couches. Some into microphones. Some to no one at all.*

*The voices do not wait for silence. They overlap, interrupt, layer on top of one another. At times, several speak at once. It is noise. It is attention. It is the sound of everyone reacting at once, and no one truly listening. MONTE is nowhere to be seen.*

CHORUS
*(layered, fragmented)*
What was he wearing? He paused too long. It felt rehearsed. It felt real. It felt like a PR move. It felt like real grief. He's so polished now. He's trying too hard. He's not trying hard enough. He used to be funnier. He only got this

CHORUS

far because of his father. He only got this far
because of his sister. He only got this far
because he's hot. Remember that one photo?

*Fog begins to fill the stage, dense and low.*

CHORUS
*(rising, layered)*
He speaks of lifting truth, but where was he
before the cameras? He's grieving. He's
broken. He's doing too much. He's not doing
enough. He's trying to be everything.

*Fog continues to build, slowly swallowing the
vignettes — like memories fading.*

CHORUS
He was born with the right face. He was raised
behind the right gates. Now he speaks of
wreckage, but continues to live beyond the
dried river. He calls for justice, but justice has
always bent his way. He wears these ruins well.

CHORUS
*(now as a loud, unified voice)*
But he looks good up there, doesn't he?

*BLACKOUT.*

*A quick silence, sharp as glass.*

*Then, a soft, warm LIGHT FADES in across the very front of the proscenium — forming a low curtain of smoke and LIGHT, like a hazy fourth wall.*

*One by one, the CHORUS re-forms, stepping through this luminous fog as if passing through a portal or waterfall.*

*As their bodies break through the smoke, they appear almost ghost-like — flickering shapes emerging from mist.*

*They move forward deliberately, each seeming to address the audience directly.*

CHORUS
*(in unison)*

We are the press. The pundits. The posters. The podcasters. The classmates. The cousins. The neighbors. The stylists. The campaign staff. The ones who liked, commented, watched... We are the Chorus of the Casanova Era.

*A final beat.*

*Unsynchronized, they all take a step back into darkness and disappear behind the curtain of smoke.*

*End of Scene.*

<h1 style="text-align:center"><u>SCENE V</u></h1>

*A white-walled studio. Sterile. Over-lit. Hushed. The lights never stop humming. MONTE stands in the middle, as a PHOTOGRAPHER hovers around him with a flashing camera.*

*Behind MONTE, a digital backdrop simulates a sweeping skyline at golden hour. The view is pristine, impossible.*

*STYLISTS and PAs hover. MONTE's ASSISTANT lingers in the corner, whispering on the phone. Further back, two CREW-MEMBERS fuss quietly with a standing fan. One tugs at a cord. The other shrugs. The machine sputters once, then goes still again. Nobody acknowledges it.*

*The camera flashes rhythmically.*

*Enter RITA HOPPER. She arrives like a silhouette someone dared to touch. Corseted, lacquered, immaculate. The makeup is a statement; the hair is architecture. She doesn't walk, she glides.*

*Her presence is erotic but untouchable, retro-futuristic, and terrifyingly composed — a voice like velvet under ice. People in the room adjust their posture before they realize she's looking.*

PHOTOGRAPHER

Little more chin. No, less. There, perfect. Now give us... bright days ahead! But bruised, a little grunge, a little secret.

*Flash. MONTE looks distant, caught in his thoughts.*

*RITA watches. Then she glides forward, heels clacking on the studio floor. She carries no notepad: just a sleek, tiny microphone-recording device and her piercing gaze.*

RITA HOPPER

Let's do the questions on the couch, shall we? I want to see how he carries comfort.
(calling out)
Can someone bring in the couch, please?
(to MONTE)
Are you okay with a couch moment, handsome?

*Two PAs enter, carrying a loveseat. MONTE
stands in silence, stunned by RITA's crudeness.
Perched with perfect posture, RITA watches the
PAs as they set the couch down.*

*As RITA and MONTE sit, another PA places a
small table beside her. She sets her mic on it,
clicks it on, then turns to MONTE and just
stares at him for a beat.*

### RITA

So, Monte. You speak well. You have charm,
charisma, the right looks... You have your
sister's cadence, yes, but... not her breath,
exactly. That's not a critique- you know what I
mean. Breath can be a liability sometimes, for
men like you.

### MONTE

Um, I thought this was a policy piece?

### RITA

It is. Society profiles are policy now. Did no
one tell you?

*One of the CREW pulls the fan cord again. The
motor coughs once, loudly, then dies.*

                    RITA

Okay, apologies if I got too excited. Let's start
fresh. Maybe a little quick back-and-forth to
break the ice? Cats or dogs?

                    MONTE

Dogs.

                    RITA

Oh, water sign?

                    MONTE

Yes?

                    RITA

Pisces?

                    MONTE

Rita, come on —

                    RITA

No, you come on, just play ball with me for a
moment. Don't you like playing with balls?

MONTE

Take it easy now...

RITA

God, I didn't know you were so sensitive.

MONTE

Just focus on the interview, please.

RITA

Okay, I'll start over, just entertain me here:
what was the last movie you watched?

MONTE

If it gets you to your point, I um... I think it was
*A Place in the Sun.*

RITA

How romantic.

MONTE

More like tragic, actually.

RITA

You or Montgomery Clift?

MONTE

The movie.

RITA

Have you seen the remake?

MONTE

Remake? *Match Point*?

RITA

Scarlett Johansson's first Cannes, I'll never forget that dress. But she's simply phenomenal in the film, so much sex appeal —

MONTE

It's not really a remake, though. It has a completely different thematic approach from the older movie.

RITA

Okay, big words.

MONTE

One is more about fate, and the other about luck.

RITA

And what are you?

MONTE

Excuse me?

RITA

Are you more about fate or luck?

MONTE

I think people rely too much on luck.

RITA

And not fate?

MONTE

I think fate is overrated.

RITA

How so?

MONTE

Ugh, you're such a pain in the ass, Rita.

MONTE

I'm just asking, do you believe in fate?

MONTE

Just cut to the chase. Can we get serious?

RITA

Okay, I'll be serious. What is it you believe in, then?

MONTE

I believe in systems. And that they're failing us.

RITA

Do you think your father failed the same way?

*A soft clatter. Someone in the back knocks something over near the fan. MONTE ignores the question by briefly looking back at the fan.*

RITA

Noted. Why don't we talk about your sister, then? My condolences, by the way. She was such an icon, really. She did so much for us. Sold us so many magazines... Truly, such a fire sign, so much heat there. And so, since you were twins, would it be safe to say you got the more, um... lukewarm genes? I mean, let's be honest here, you drift around everything. And sure, you do it beautifully, but —

MONTE
*(interrupting)*
Rita, just ask what you came here for —

*BANG! A loud noise in the back: the fan roars to life in the highest setting. A full blast of wind hits MONTE mid-sentence.*

*His shirt flies open, caught like a sail. His chest
is briefly exposed — lean, toned, defined.*

*He flinches instinctively, and two PAs rush in.
One gently presses his shirt back down. The
other untangles a microphone wire from his
side.*

                    RITA
           *(feigned innocence, provoking)*
Are you okay to continue or do you need some
fog for added drama —

                   MONTE
      *(measured calm, just shy of condescending)*
Let's just go back to the interview.

*MONTE'S ASSISTANT signals to the CREW
and they power down the fan. Silence returns.*

                    RITA
So... Do you think this initiative of yours will
succeed? These revolutionary plans of yours to
bring back "the truth", peace, or... whatever, to
our lovely City of Angels.

MONTE

Well, thank you for bringing that up. The plan
my team and I have laid out is actually very
special to me. We carefully reviewed our
current District policies and identified the
public sectors that fail to —

*RITA breaks into laughter. It's sudden, sharp.
MONTE stops mid-sentence, thrown off.*

*She exhales a long sigh, then looks at him in
silence. Slowly, she reaches for her recording
device and clicks off.*

RITA
*(softly)*

Do you really think anyone cares about your
opinions on policy?

*A beat. MONTE looks around. He doesn't
answer. She leans in — her voice low, close,
like a threat.*

RITA

Listen, kid, you're giving me nothing here.
Come on, no one wants you to be the big hero.
People want passion! Heat! Something they'll
want to watch twice! Now get your shit
together, and don't waste my time.

*MONTE says nothing. RITA clicks the
microphone back on and leans back. Her smile
returns, perfect and distant.*

RITA
*(returning)*

Monte. Our adorable and handsome Monte. We
just want to get to know you better. Tell us
about that speechwriter friend of yours?
Anything juicy over there?

*MONTE opens his mouth, but he stops himself
from voicing his first thoughts. After a beat:*

MONTE
*(calm)*

I'm not doing this, Rita. You can leave.

*A faint glitch stutters across the digital
backdrop.*

*RITA doesn't move; she stares at him in silence
for a moment. She then exhales and adjusts her
gloves; she's over it. RITA stands up and walks
off stage.*

*The studio stays LIT. The crew stays quiet. MONTE sits there still. Alone. Tired, staring at the silence.*

*LIGHTS FADE.*

*End of Scene.*

<h1 style="text-align:center"><u>SCENE VI</u></h1>

*A motel room in the outer edges of the city.
Sparse. Still.*

*Rain taps softly on the window and against the
rusted air unit outside. Not a storm — just the
kind of steady, greasy rain that makes a city
feel like it's sweating.*

*A TV hums in the corner, playing an old movie
on low volume. The dialogue is distant.
Unimportant. On the floor: a neon ball. A robot
dog blinks beside it, sleek and quiet, almost too
still.*

*MONTE sits cross-legged on the floor. He
lazily tosses the ball across the room. The dog
fetches it, brings it back, and drops it again. It's
a repeating cycle. He doesn't smile.*

*MONTE drinks from a half-full beer bottle and
places it on a book used as a coaster beside him
on the ground.*

*A knock on the door. Light, intentionally soft.
MONTE doesn't answer.*

*A pause. Then the door opens with a soft scrape. Enter NICO.*
*Rain clings to his boots, his coat, his hair. His shoulders are dotted with it. He closes the door quietly. Doesn't look at MONTE yet.*

*He shrugs off his coat, still damp, speaking as he does.*

NICO

Nice place. Very... analog of you.

*He tosses the coat onto the back of a chair, bends to undo one boot, his movements automatic.*

MONTE
(still seated, not looking)

It's quiet.

NICO

You and the dog doing press together?

*NICO kicks off the first boot, straightens up, and finally gives MONTE a look.*

*MONTE tosses the ball and pulls a vape out of
his pocket. The robot dog dashes after it,
returns, drops it again. MONTE takes a hit.*
                    MONTE
                  (deadpan)
Yeah, but gets way better coverage than me.


*MONTE sips his beer. NICO moves farther in,
loosens the second boot, setting it aside.
MONTE tosses the ball again and offers NICO
the vape, which NICO accepts with a nod.*


*The dog runs, retrieves the ball, and returns.
NICO takes a hit of the vape and coughs
dramatically. They both laugh, and the tension
lightens for a moment.*


                    NICO
              *(nodding at the robot)*
What's his name?


                    MONTE
Dude.


*A pause.*


                    NICO
She used to call you that.

*MONTE looks down at the dog as it plays with the ball.*

*The TV murmurs in the background, dialogue muffled. NICO takes another hit of the vape and passes it back to MONTE.*


MONTE

She thought there was still time. That, if we came out with a clear plan, people would listen.


NICO

Was she wrong?


*A pause. MONTE hits the vape again and gives it to NICO.*


MONTE

No, she wasn't built for this. The noise. The theater. The whole acting-like-you're-not-acting bit.


*NICO takes a hit and continues, lightly stoned:*


NICO

Yeah. Kind of like that one opera we saw in New York —

MONTE
*(letting out a soft chuckle)*
Oh my God, with the crazy big masks!
NICO
They were so dramatic.


MONTE
What was that one line —


NICO
*(dramatically yelling)*
CYPHER, YOU TRAITOR! NO!


*They laugh at NICO's bad acting.*
MONTE
It was so bad, they literally copied the entire
plot twist from *The Matrix*.


NICO
Okay, but I kinda liked it.


MONTE
Cypher? A betrayal "no one saw coming"?
Come on, how original...


NICO
Maybe it's not about being original, but it's
about proving a point.

MONTE
(*mocking, like it's an in-joke*)
Okay, fire sign.


NICO
Ugh, shut up. I don't know, I just... I think just I
understood his reasoning for the whole bit —


*Pause. They look at each other.*


MONTE
That's worse.


*They break out in laughter. The robot dog trots
over with the ball, drops it at MONTE's feet.
He tosses it across the room. The laughter fades
to a softer hum between them.*


NICO
You're right... You were always better at
playing the part.


*MONTE doesn't look up, but his body shifts.*


NICO
You know how to make things look clean. Like
everything is going to be okay... Even if just for
a second.

*MONTE finally looks at him. There's no defensiveness in his face, just a tired kind of knowing.*

MONTE

Well, it's one thing to make things look better. It's another to make things right.

*He takes a sip of the beer. Silence.*

*Dude sits quietly near the bed, tail glowing faintly.*

MONTE

You ever feel like if you stop pretending for even just a second, the whole world would fall apart?

NICO

Yeah...

*A pause.*

NICO
(whispering)
But I didn't get a stage for it.

*MONTE flinches a little and places the beer on the floor beside him.*

MONTE

Why are you acting like this? You've been so hot and cold lately, judging me, picking on me. You think I'm enjoying all of this? This isn't a show, this is my life. Trinity was my sister. This isn't a stage, are you kidding me, it's all a fucking trap door —

NICO
*(sharper now, but contained)*
Yeah, well, you fell through and still got your flowers. I didn't get a mask for my grief, I had to keep walking through it.

*A pause. MONTE's eyes lift. The silence is louder than the rain.*

MONTE
*(low)*
You think I wanted all this attention?

*A beat.*

NICO
The world gave it to you anyway.

*A long silence lingers. Almost too long. They
both look away from each other. MONTE takes
a sip of his beer.*


NICO

I'm sorry. Long day —


MONTE

Do you remember that night? Right after she
died. I couldn't get out of bed. I thought... I
don't know, I couldn't even move.


*The rain presses against the window. NICO
doesn't interrupt.*


MONTE

And you came over. You didn't say anything.
You just... put water on the stove. Made some
tea. Sat on the floor with me.


NICO
*(turning to MONTE)*
I stayed all night. You didn't have to say a
word.


*MONTE looks at NICO.*

                    NICO

Next morning you were on the news.


                   MONTE

I had to be. Someone had to smile.


*The rain softens.*


                   MONTE
              *(sitting back, voice low)*
Sometimes I think they want to stay broken. It's
easier than facing what they had to give up.


*NICO doesn't respond.*


                   MONTE
                *(after a beat)*
They fell for the smile. The promise. They'd
vote for a mirror if it flattered them.


                    NICO

Is that what your father was?


                   MONTE
               *(almost a whisper)*
I think he wanted to help. But they didn't want
help. They wanted to feel safe.

*A silence. Dude nudges the ball again. MONTE doesn't move.*

MONTE
*(more to himself)*
No matter what I say, they'll always turn on me.

NICO
*(gently)*
So, what now?

MONTE
I don't know. Maybe I disappear. Go somewhere no one knows me. Work a job that pays the rent. Live a life that doesn't need saving.

*He looks at NICO. There's no performance in his face.*

NICO
*(soft)*
You'd leave all this behind?

MONTE
Wouldn't you?

*A long silence. The rain picks back up.*

NICO

Get some rest.


*MONTE nods faintly. Doesn't speak.*


*NICO stands. Crosses the room. Picks up his coat. He doesn't look back. He opens the door, and Dude shifts but doesn't bark. The door clicks shut behind him.*


*The room holds still. The TV screen glows faintly.*


*Monte stares into nothing.*


*End of Act I.*

# ACT II

## <u>SCENE VII</u>

*A high-rise apartment, glass-walled and cold.
Outside: a digital skyline flickering through
light rain. Inside: soft-lit screens, an open
laptop, half-eaten takeout. The room hums with
quiet dread. Phones buzz.*

*Center stage: a large TV monitor plays a live
news stream. A slick, composed female
journalist in a red suit delivers commentary.*

*The journalist speaks with sharp, deliberate
diction:*

*"In newly leaked audio, Monte Casanova
appears to call voters 'dumb,' a fatal blow to a
figure already accused of entitlement, vanity,
and disconnect. The leak is damning not
because it surprises anyone, but because it
confirms what so many feared: that beneath the
polish, there was always contempt."*

*The sound fades under. MONTE enters. He
looks good. Too good. Dressed sharp. Hair
styled. He hasn't seen the footage yet.*

MONTE

What's the damage?


*Silence. One advisor looks up from their tablet, startled. Another just shakes their head.*


ADVISOR 1

They have you on audio. Everyone has it.
*MONTE takes off his jacket and sets it on a chair nearby.*


MONTE

Where did this break first?


ADVISOR 2

*AltNet.* Then *The State Stream.* Then everywhere. People thought it was satire at first, but...


*A phone buzzes. No one moves to answer.*


MONTE

But?


*From the TV, the leaked audio faintly plays:*

MONTE
(TV audio)
"I'll take the money and disappear."

*They all look at the screen. MONTE quickly
mutes the TV before the audio continues.*

MONTE
What the fuck is that?

*Silence.*
MONTE
(confused, then piecing it together)
Is that from...

*His tone shifts. He gets it.*

MONTE
(angry)
It's from the motel.

*One advisor stutters.*

MONTE
I'm so confused, I... That's not what I was
saying —

ADVISOR 1

We can still shape this. Maybe an apology.
Brief, but real. Say you were misquoted.
Emotional. Overwhelmed.


MONTE

No, no, I didn't say that —


ADVISOR 2

Monte, come on, it's us —


MONTE

Someone must have spliced that together. I'm
not going out there to confirm a lie.


ADVISOR 2

You're not confirming anything. Just a few
remarks. A little teary-eyed moment and...


MONTE

You want me to cry?


ADVISOR 2

I want them to like you.


*A pause. MONTE turns toward the monitor.*

MONTE
(dryly)

Oh, they're really going to love this one...

An intern stands in the corner, watching but silent. MONTE notices.

MONTE
(to intern)

Do you believe it?

INTERN

I believe that red suit's about to sell out.

MONTE walks to the window. The skyline outside glitches faintly. A distant siren wails. He lets out a soft, ironic chuckle.

MONTE
(whispers)

Does anyone care?

He turns to the room.

MONTE

Why should I care? They just want someone to yell at.

*Silence. Then someone rushes in: MONTE'S
ASSISTANT.*

## ASSISTANT

Time out, boys. The press is about to surround
this building. Monte, you're out of here.

## MONTE

And where am I going?

## ASSISTANT

You can figure that out in the elevator, your car
is waiting downstairs.

*MONTE stays still for a beat — frozen,
processing.*

*He grabs his coat from the back of the chair
and rushes out the door.*

*No one says a word.*

*LIGHTS FADE.*

*End of Scene.*

<u>**SCENE VIII**</u>

*A dim sanctuary. Candles flicker in half-spent rows. A dusty organ looms in the shadows. The stained glass is cracked, bleeding colored LIGHT across the floor.*

*A single figure, the PRIEST, tends to a candle. Footsteps echo. MONTE enters quietly. He watches for a beat. Then speaks.*

MONTE

They said you still answer when people knock. Wasn't sure if that was a metaphor or marketing.

PRIEST
*(without turning)*

Both.

MONTE

You always this poetic, or is it just me?

PRIEST
*(turning to MONTE)*

Only when the silence demands it. You look tired.

MONTE

I am. But I've been sleeping more than ever and... Honestly? Feels worse.

*The PRIEST tends to another candle, doesn't say anything.*

MONTE

It's not insomnia, it's... rest without peace?

PRIEST

Peace is not the absence of noise, Monte, but the presence of understanding.

MONTE

Then I am in turmoil.

PRIEST

Echoes can guide us, if we listen. They carry the truths we often ignore.

MONTE

Well, I came here seeking answers, not riddles.

PRIEST

Sometimes, answers come wrapped in riddles.

MONTE

Well then, what if I don't get it? What if I...
What if I failed?


PRIEST

Failure is not in falling, son. But in refusing to
rise.


*MONTE lets out a chuckle. He strolls down the
aisle.*


MONTE

I don't know what I'm supposed to do anymore.


PRIEST

Stop chasing what you think people want from
you, Monte. You want to be loud and crash the
system? Scream. You want to run away? Run.
But whatever it is, make sure it's yours. Make
sure it's for you.


MONTE

And if it destroys everything?


PRIEST

That's quite dramatic, but... Even then, at least
it was honest, no?

MONTE

Maybe. I think I'm... tired of trying to make sense through everyone else's lens.


PRIEST

It's your peace to find. No one else's.


MONTE

Even if it risks starting over?


PRIEST

Especially if you have to start over.


*MONTE looks at the PRIEST, turns, and starts walking out.*

MONTE

Thanks.


*MONTE exits.*


*The candles flicker. A distant sound begins to swell: muffled chanting and a low beat like boots or drums. the PRIEST stays standing, but his tone shifts.*

PRIEST (AS CHORUS)

He left this place lighter. Not because he was saved, but because he believed the weight could be shared. But outside, they weren't seeking the truth. They were preparing the stage. For headlines. For consequences. For blood that wouldn't stain their own hands. The leak was only a signal. The outrage was engineered. The protest, arranged. The humiliation, deliberate. But what came next wasn't part of the plan.

*The chanting builds to a roar. An orchestral impact. The candles go out: BLACKOUT.*

*End of Scene.*

# <u>SCENE IX</u>

*Exterior of MONTE's apartment building. Urban cold. The LIGHT outside is digital blue, washed and flickering, as if the city is thinking in pixels. A soft drizzle. Thunder murmurs above. Every so often, a FLICKER of distant lightning.*

*A crowd has gathered: some in ponchos, some under umbrellas, some soaking without care. Protest signs rise and fall in the shifting dark. A few news cameras wait, still, expectant.*

*A LIGHT divides interior from exterior.*

*MONTE steps into view, crossing the threshold. A DOORMAN holds the door open behind him. As MONTE steps out, phones rise like a reflex. A few boos. Shouts.*

*Monte steps just past the threshold. He's calm.*

### MONTE

I know what you've heard, what they cut together. I didn't say any of that. I'm not here to ask for anything, just —

*The crowd yells over him.*

CROWD MEMBER

We heard the tape!

*A sharp crack — the sound of glass fracturing. One of the side windows has been hit. We don't see the impact. Only the sound. MONTE holds his ground. The crowd jolts, then half-cheers.*

MONTE

Breaking shit isn't going to fix anything. Listen to me, someone set me up —

*Then: an object flies from the crowd. Fast. Dirty. Improvised. It spins once, hurtling toward MONTE.*

*A blinding flash — the HOUSE LIGHTS burst on for a split second.*

*A thunderous explosion.*

*Instant BLACKOUT.*

*Shouts. Scramble. Glass. Chaos in the dark.*

*End of Scene.*

### <u>SCENE X</u>

*A spacious hotel suite. Brutalist and severe. Muted gray and blue tones. Velvet furniture, heavy carpet. Heavy curtains drawn tight. A desk near the window. A single lamp casts a low pool of LIGHT.*

*MONTE sits at the desk, writing. His back is to the audience. The room is silent.*

*The door opens. NICO enters. A soft click behind him.*

MONTE

You shouldn't have come.

*He does not turn.*

NICO

I had to... You disappeared. I didn't know if you —

*He stops himself. Silence.*

*MONTE turns slowly. His face is fully bandaged, except for his eyes and mouth — clean, tight, almost surgical. A figure halfway between a patient and a ghost.*

NICO

Fuck. I didn't know what to expect. I thought
maybe you'd be... I don't know —

MONTE

Better?

NICO

Something. Anything that looked like... you.

*A pause. MONTE doesn't say anything. NICO
crosses a small distance, but doesn't get close.*

NICO

Can I sit?

*MONTE doesn't answer. NICO sits.*

NICO

There's something I need to tell you. And I
don't know how to say it without sounding like
I'm trying to make it better. But I'm not. I just
want you to know what I did.

*Silence.*

NICO

The leak... That was me. I recorded it. At the
motel.

*A beat. MONTE's gaze stays fixed.*

NICO

I spliced it. Sent it out. Paid to push it. It wasn't supposed to go this far, I...

*Silence.*

MONTE
*(whispering)*

You were quiet that night. When you walked in.

NICO

What?

MONTE

I remember thinking you weren't yourself. Now I know why.

*A beat.*

MONTE

You didn't ruin me. You just made it easier for everyone else to finish the job.

NICO

I thought if you fell, they'd need someone to step in. Someone quieter. Hungrier. Willing to go the distance.

                    MONTE
Willing to go the distance?


                    NICO
You stopped following the script, Monte —


                    MONTE
And you thought you could do it better.


                    NICO
Oh, I know I can. I wrote everything you ever
said. Everything you ever pretended to believe
in. I created you.


                    MONTE
You don't get to walk away clean. Not from
this. They'll hand you the mic. They'll hand you
the power. But you'll spend every night waiting
for someone to do to you what you did to me.


*MONTE rises and steps closer.*


                    MONTE
And the worst part? You'll carry it forever.
Long after the applause. Long after the screens
go dark and the rooms are empty. You'll carry
it in every silence. Every mirror. In every
person who smiles at you without meaning it.

MONTE

You'll carry it in the quiet mornings, when no one is watching. And that's when it will weigh the most.

*He steps even closer — his voice low, almost gentle now.*

MONTE

So take it. Take the attention. Take the headlines. Take the seat. Take the crown. Take everything that was built on my collapse.

*Silence.*

MONTE

But don't mistake power for peace. What's yours will come. And when it does, may it be heavy.

NICO

I didn't mean for it to happen like this. I thought —

MONTE

You thought you'd rise from my ashes —

NICO

No, listen to me, I think we can still make this work —

MONTE<br>
(cutting Nico off)

Shut up!

Silence.

MONTE

You can leave. I never want to see you again.
I'm done with all of this. And I'm done with
you.

NICO rises slowly. He doesn't respond. He
lingers a second too long, like he wants to say
something else but doesn't. He walks to the
door. Opens it.

A slice of hallway LIGHT cuts across the room
— a sharp line between NICO and MONTE.

NICO looks back. Then exits. The door closes
quietly behind him.

MONTE remains still. The silence returns.

MONTE

They will say I was too much. Too loud, too
proud, too fragile, too angry. They will say that
I cracked under pressure. But they won't say

MONTE

why. You stand in the fire long enough, and
they stop asking what you're burning for. They
just watch. And when the ash settles, they
pretend they never saw you at all.

*A pause. He exhales.*

MONTE

But maybe that's the point. To stand anyway,
even if no one's left to see you. But if no one's
watching, is any of it real?

*A low orchestral swell begins to rise, barely
audible at first. A single string note, distant and
tense, begins to hum beneath his voice. As
MONTE continues, the music swells gradually,
mournful, growing.*

MONTE

Kind of like the age-old question of
immaterialism: if an object sits in a room but no
one's there to see it, how do we know the object
exists? Well, news flash: centuries later, we're
still haunted by that philosophical doubt. It
consumes all of us. We gather, we yell, we
plead... so afraid that stillness will bring

MONTE

something to an end. We mistake surveillance for care, and attention for love

*A pause.*

MONTE

They will wonder what happened. Why did he disappear? Did he break? Did he finally give up? They'll name my weaknesses. They'll call it madness. But the truth is much simpler. I chose to stop explaining myself. Silence over nonsense. And this silence, this... refusal, is the loudest thing I've ever done.

*MONTE returns to the desk. He picks up his pen and writes one more line. The music peaks the moment his pen lands on the paper.*

*BLACKOUT.*

*Silence.*

*End of Scene.*

## <u>SCENE XI</u>

*The stage is dark. Faint crackling of fire. A distant siren. Two pairs of footsteps over debris — slow, cautious.*


OFFICER

Looks like it started in the corner. Maybe electrical?


DETECTIVE

Or not... You smell that?


*They continue walking over debris. We hear the scrape of a chair being nudged aside, the hollow clatter of a box shifting, the dull thud of a lamp hitting the floor. Something fragile falls — a crash — then the soft, unsettling sound of ashes spreading across tile.*


*LIGHTS SLOWLY FADE IN. We see the same hotel suite from before, now scorched and almost unrecognizable. The desk is half-melted, and the curtains blackened. Light ash drifts through the air like dust.*


*Two men, an OFFICER and a DETECTIVE, move carefully through the debris in gloves, stepping over rubble. They sift through the wreckage — lifting a fallen chair, opening a scorched drawer, brushing ash off a shattered lamp. A soft crunch echoes underfoot.*

*The DETECTIVE takes a slow drag from a thin electronic cigarette.*

OFFICER

Clothes were here. Shoes too. All charred to hell. But no body.

*The DETECTIVE steps on a photo frame — the glass cracks.*

OFFICER

Press is calling it a tragedy. Whole campaign up in smoke.

DETECTIVE
*(exhaling smoke)*

I don't give a fuck about the press. Has anyone tracked down that Nico kid who's always with him? Where is he?

OFFICER
(*checking phone*)
Sorry, sir, looks like my guys got caught up in
something by the river.


DETECTIVE
Should probably start the paperwork then.


OFFICER
You want to arrest him?


DETECTIVE
Receptionist says he was the last one here. Now
he's gone missing? I'm not wasting any —


*MONTE'S ASSISTANT enters quickly. They're
pale, clutching a phone.*


ASSISTANT
They found him. Nico.


*The ASSISTANT shows the phone screen to the
OFFICER. We never see it. The OFFICER
recoils — just slightly.*


*The DETECTIVE crosses, takes the phone. He
studies it in silence. Then hands it back.*

OFFICER

Holy shit.


*The DETECTIVE just stares at the fire damage.*


ASSISTANT

It says here he had weights attached to his feet.
God, I —

DETECTIVE
*(exhaling smoke)*

Go home, kid.


*Silence. A faint wind brushes through the space.
The burnt curtains stir slightly. The ASSISTANT
hesitates, eyes glassy. They linger, scanning the
wreckage, then crouch to pick something from
the ash — a charred wristwatch.*


*They hold it for a moment, turning it in their
palm. Fingers close around it.*


ASSISTANT
*(letting out a fond chuckle)*

He was terrified of running out of time.


*The ASSISTANT looks up at the DETECTIVE.*

ASSISTANT

Can I keep this?


*The DETECTIVE meets their eyes, says nothing. He takes another slow drag from the thin electronic cigarette, exhales, and gives a small, deliberate nod.*


*The ASSISTANT slips the watch into their pocket and turns to leave. Their footsteps fade into the silence.*

OFFICER

So, what now?

DETECTIVE

I guess we can wrap this up and open a new case for the river.


*The OFFICER pulls out his phone and starts taking notes.*

OFFICER

You don't think they're connected?

DETECTIVE
*(low)*

Maybe by fate...

OFFICER

What was that?


DETECTIVE

Nothing. I mean, sure. Makes sense for the kid to go all Frank Underwood on Prince Charming over here. Maybe get a nice promotion. New office, bigger apartment... But why go the distance only to drown yourself right after, I'm just... Not so sure anymore... But the fire! The fire definitely came from inside... Feels almost planned —


OFFICER
*(still taking notes)*

So two suicides then...


DETECTIVE
*(interrupting)*

Wait. Hold on.


*They both stop. The DETECTIVE exhales smoke, his gaze fixed on the OFFICER with a sudden, heavier tone. The OFFICER stops typing, confused. A beat passes — the air feels heavier.*

DETECTIVE

Maybe just note one for now.

*Pause. The OFFICER glances around the charred room, uneasy.*

DETECTIVE

Let's get out of here.

*They begin walking toward the exit, slow, deliberate. As the LIGHTS start to FADE, the DETECTIVE's voice cuts softly through the dark.*

DETECTIVE

Hope you don't mind a little water...

*BLACKOUT.*

*End of Scene.*

<h1 style="text-align:center"><u>SCENE XII</u></h1>

*LIGHTS rise slowly on center stage.*

*The PRIEST emerges from darkness, walking in silence. He carries a long, draping funeral arrangement: white lilies and dark green branches. Woven through the stems is a soft sash that reads: "Per sempre tuo, Monte Casanova" (Forever yours, Monte Casanova).*

*The PRIEST takes his place center stage, facing forward. Still, upright.*

*One by one, other CHORUS MEMBERS begin to step forward from the edges of the stage. Phones in hand again — like fireflies emerging from the darkness.*

*They walk in silence and join the PRIEST, forming a square reminiscent of the play's opening formation. Each one stands upright, gazing outward, into the horizon line.*

*As they take their places, they begin to speak — not separately, but as one voice.*

CHORUS:
We saw the night split in two.
Smoke rose to the stars.
The river swallowed the moon.
Neither asked for permission.

Fire runs, and it does not wait.
It devours everything but the shape of what it
loved.
Water waits.
It washes all things away, and nothing returns
the same.

Some vanish in the blaze,
leaving only the outline of their last step.
Others vanish in the current,
their names pulled under before we can speak
them.

But fire and water are never finished.
They wait at the edge of every choice.
In the rooms we enter,
In the silences we keep.

One will ask you to burn for what you believe.
One will ask you to drift, disappear.
Neither forgives.
Both will call your name.

CHORUS:

And when they do,
you must choose.
Wait too long,
and the fire leaves nothing to choose from.
The tide does not ask twice.

The path will not always be clear.
Sometimes you must take the leap.
Say what you have kept unsaid,
even when the ground shakes.

And when the air tastes of smoke and rain,
remember: the sky won't break.
A new story begins every second.
And now, somewhere not far from here,
someone is still deciding where to stand.

If you had the chance to start over,
where would you go next?

*As the last words of the monologue hang in the air, the CHORUS holds its formation for a suspended beat — only the sound of breathing in the dim LIGHT.*

*One by one, they step back into the shadows, phone screens dimming as they disappear.*

*As the CHORUS dissolves, one figure remains still among them. With each person who drifts into darkness, his outline sharpens — until it's clear: MONTE stands at center stage.*

*MONTE stands in a plain white T-shirt, unzipped black hoodie, jeans, and scuffed Converse shoes. A suitcase hangs loosely at his side.*

*The deep roar of an approaching subway train swells in the distance, growing louder. Then a rush of air stirs his hair and clothes, a strong wind cutting through the stillness.*

*MONTE lets a faint, knowing smile cross his face as the sound peaks. A split second later:*

*BLACKOUT. Immediate silence.*

*A recorded subway voice plays:*

*"Stand clear of the closing doors, please."*

*END OF PLAY.*

About the Author

Tutafarel is the creative alias of Raphael
Rosalen, a Brazilian artist and writer based in
Los Angeles, CA. His work blends music,
literature, and digital media. *Monte Casanova* is
his debut play, released alongside his first
album of the same name.